I dedicate this book to my 3 children. Hadley and Zeke, who I am blessed to raise each day. To my Harper girl who is in heaven, I know we will meet again.
You are my heroes.

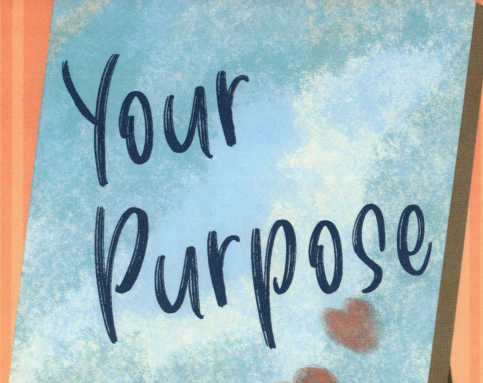

Your Purpose

Jenny Loomis

illustrated by
Mousam Banerjee

All children have stories of courage and love,

given by our Creator who lives above.

my body needs extra help
and most of all
loved one's cheer

It can be hard to find the words to say,

I need to take my time and I will get better each day.

Sometimes I am sick and do not feel well,
I need to be patient and listen to what my body tells.

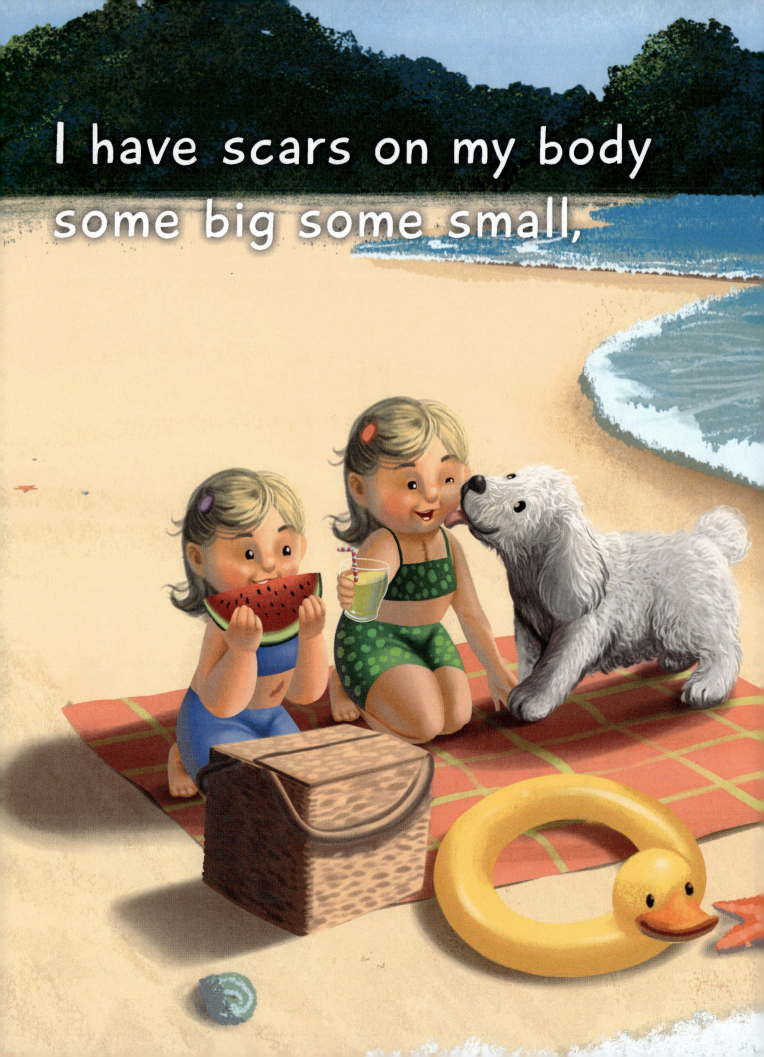

scars tell a story of healing for us all.

Once in a while I need help from machines,
it aides me to become healthy so I can fulfill my dreams.

We are all God's children who have purpose,

About the Author

Jenny Loomis lives in Arvada, Colorado with her two children Hadley and Zeke. She has her bachelor's degree and teaching license in early childhood education. Jenny and the kids enjoy outdoor activities and spending time with family and friends. Jenny lost her daughter, Harper-Hadley's twin sister, to a congenital heart defect 10 days after birth. Her daughter Hadley was diagnosed a few years later with a rare chromosomal malfunction. Through Hadley's progress and medical trials Jenny relied on her faith, family, and friends. Her son Zeke has been Hadley's encourager. He has helped her tremendously with her confidence and progress.

Jenny wants to encourage children to view obstacles as their strength. All children, even in their limitations, have a God given purpose.

About the illustrator

Mousam Banerjee is a full time artist and illustrator who loves painting whimsical children's books to realistic concept art. Born in an artistic family in India, he was keen on creating original paintings right from childhood.
With a Post Graduate Diploma in Fine arts, he has now made a career in Digital illustrations. He has worked a lot of published Children's Books, Book Covers and Concept designs.
You can find him on www.illus-station.com

Note from the Author

"After three months of being in the NICU with Hadley and hearing whispers of different labels and diagnoses; there were moments when I did not know what Hadley's life was going to look like. Through prayer, God humbly took me out of my fear and preconceived expectations. I realized Hadley has a purpose no matter what her impairment; just as Harper has a purpose in the 10 days she was with us. I had this overwhelming peace in accepting my babies exactly how God created them even in their limitations.

I learned to cherish the time I have with my children, celebrating every success, and being patient with their progress. I learned when it was time to challenge Hadley, when it was time for rest, and when it was time for play. Over time, she has found her confidence, strength, and independence. She has exceeded all expectations. Each of us has a unique purpose to share with others. I am honored to watch my children discover their purpose."

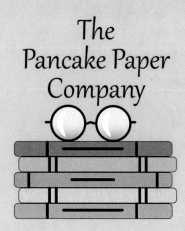

This book was formatted and published to Kindle Direct Publishing through The Pancake Paper Company.

If you're interested in learning more about our book coaching services, and how to self-publish your own book, contact us at tppc17@gmail.com .

Made in the USA
Monee, IL
07 July 2023